Adapted by Jasmine Jones

Based on the series created by

Mark McCorkle & Bob Schooley

New York

Library of Congress Catalog Card Number: 2003096537

ISBN 0-7868-4625-9

For more Disney Press fun, visit www.disneybooks.com
Visit DisneyChannel.com

CHAPTER 1

Kim's Cam-Pain

"Listen up, people!" Mr. Barkin bellowed. The teacher stood on the stage in the auditorium in his usual brown suit, his hands clasped behind his back. With his military-style crew cut and his deep voice, he looked and sounded like a general addressing his troops. "The time has come to choose Middleton High's new student government."

Kim Possible leaned forward in her chair eagerly. True, she was already a teenage superhero, but it wasn't exactly something you could put on a college application. "Class president," on the other hand . . .

"Class president is . . . a magnificent burden," Mr. Barkin said. "An excruciating

 opportunity. Now . . . let's have some nominations for this glorious, thankless task."

The auditorium was silent, well, except for the guy in the third row, who was snoring his head off.

Mr. Barkin frowned. "This is a democracy, people," he growled. "Now do as I say. Let's hear some nominations!"

Kim elbowed her best friend, Ron Stoppable, who was sitting next to her, completely spaced out.

"Huh?" Ron said, blinking at Kim.

Back in third period, Ron had agreed to nominate her—but he had clearly forgotten all about it. Kim rolled her eyes and gestured toward the stage.

"Oh!" Ron cried, leaping to his feet. "Mr. Barkin, from the great state of confusion, I am proud to nominate our next class president, Kim Possible."

Ron's pet naked mole rat, Rufus, popped out of Ron's pocket. "Second!" Rufus squeaked. He was a pretty smart mole rat.

Whipping out a large plastic horn, Ron blew an obnoxious honk. Rufus, who was wearing a little hat and waving a flag bearing the letters "K.P.," tooted a horn too.

Ron plopped back into his chair with a self-satisfied sigh. "Done and done, K.P."

Kim's eyebrows drew together. "Ron, I wanted to run for class president, not class clown," she said.

"Suit yourself," Ron said with a shrug. "Clowns have more fun."

Mr. Barkin scanned the crowd of students. "Challengers?"

Bonnie Rockwaller shot out of her seat. "I nominate Brick Flagg," she called, pointing to the quarterback of the football team.

"What?" Kim cried as she stared at Bonnie. Bonnie and Kim were on the cheer squad together, and it seemed that Bonnie was always trying to steal Kim's thunder.

Brick pulled his headphones away from his ears. "What?" he asked. He had no idea what was going on. Kim wondered if he even knew where he was. Brick was about as bright as a burned-out lightbulb in a blackout.

"The cheerleader versus the quarterback," Mr. Barkin said with a smile. "Classic."

"Don't worry, K.P.," Ron said quickly.

"Brick Flagg may be the most popular jock in school, but you have something he doesn't." Ron wiggled his eyebrows. "You've got Ron Stoppable as your campaign manager."

Kim slumped down in her seat. "Great."

CHAPTER 2

Kickin' It
Wally Style

"Imagine the ball going not only into the Eiffel Tower, but through it," Ron said to Kim as he gazed at the third hole at Middleton Mini-Golf.

"What does this have to do with my campaign?" Kim demanded. "Bonnie's probably painted dozens of 'Pick Brick' posters by now."

Ron rolled his eyes toward the sky and sighed. "Kim, duh. The best political strategies are figured out on the golf course," he said, as though he were explaining the most obvious thing in the world. "Now let's move on to Old Faithful, shall we?" he suggested, pointing to the obstacle on the fourth hole.

"I don't care about the big political deals," Kim insisted. "I want to help the people."

Ron waved at her dismissively. "Kim, you're going to have to cut out this 'serious' thing if you want to beat Brick," he said. "Voters hate that. Oh, and maybe you should get a dog. Voters like dogs."

Suddenly, Kim's Kimmunicator chirped.

Kim pulled it from her pocket and looked at the screen. "What's the sitch, Wade?"

Wade, the ten-year-old computer genius who ran Kim's Web site,

appeared on the screen. He could hack into anything, which came in pretty handy. "We got a hit from His Majesty, King Wallace," Wade explained.

Kim frowned. "And should I know who that is?" she asked.

"He rules a tiny European nation," Wade said.

"How tiny?" Ron asked.

"The Middleton Mall is more crowded," Wade told them. He took a sip of water, then went on. "Anyway, he has a son, Prince Wally, who needs your help."

That was all Kim needed to hear.

* * *

A little while later, Kim and Ron arrived at the airport.

"They sent the royal jet?" Kim said as she eyed the white plane. "Spankin'!"

Ron stopped cold in the middle of the tarmac. "As campaign manager, I must veto this mission," he announced. "This whole 'helping' thing," he said, using his fingers as quotation marks, "is definitely not 'helping' you in the polls."

A corner of Kim's mouth twitched up into a smile. "What polls?"

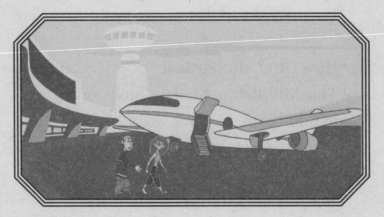

"These two guys I talk to in the caf," Ron said, jerking his thumb in the direction of the school cafeteria. Which, by the way, was miles away.

Kim yanked Ron toward the plane. She had bigger problems than the two guys in the caf. "Let's worry about my poll numbers later," she said.

After a luxurious flight, Kim and Ron got into a royal limousine, which took them to an ancient stone palace that stood at the top of a hill, overlooking the peaceful green countryside below. I'll say one thing about the monarchies in tiny European countries, Kim thought as she and Ron stepped out of the limo. They sure have style!

Just then, a slim, pale, large-eared boy

13

about Kim's age bounded out of the palace. He was dressed in a double-breasted blazer and a purple tie. "Whassup, homey homes!" he said in a snooty-sounding accent. "I'm your main dude brother man and such."

"Uh . . . hello," Kim said, stepping forward. She had a feeling this was Prince Wallace. But somehow, he wasn't quite as . . . *princely* as she had expected. "I'm Kim, and this is Ron."

"Tut, tut, tut!" Prince Wallace said. He squinted, shading his eyes with his hand. "Hold that thought . . . and if you could sidestep just a smidge. Sun in my eyes."

"I'm on it," Ron said eagerly.

Kim held up her hand. "Wait a second, Ron. Uh, Wally . . ."

"'Royal Highness,' if it's all the same," Wally corrected her.

Kim gritted her teeth. This prince was certainly *not* charming. "Couldn't you just move over a few inches?" she suggested. "Royal Highness."

"Well, if I fancied to move, I suppose I could," Wally said.

"But . . . you don't fancy," Kim finished, scowling.

Suddenly, a trumpet sounded and a handsome older man walked out of the palace. He was wearing a white jacket with a brightly colored sash across the front. If there was any doubt that this was the king, it disappeared when Wally's eyes grew round and he squealed, "Daddy!"

Ron stepped forward and gave a low bow. "King Wallace," he said solemnly. "Dude."

Rufus skittered onto Ron's head and bowed low. "Hi," Rufus chirped.

"Kim Possible," King Wallace said, ignoring Ron. His voice was rich and deep. "Welcome to our kingdom."

"We are here for you, Your Majesty," Ron said, shaking the king's hand. "'Your

Majesty.'" Ron giggled, pointing to the king. "How cool is that?"

"You must be Wade!" King Wallace cried, patting Ron on the back. "The super genius who runs Kim's Web site."

"Uh, no. I'm Ron," Ron corrected. "Ron Stoppable? Sidekick."

"Oh," the king said, clearly disappointed. "I've never heard of you."

Ron nodded. "Right, mm-hm," he said. "That's because I prefer to, you know, work behind the scenes. I do all the important—"

"Mmm," King Wallace interrupted Ron. "Miss Possible, could I speak to you privately?"

"Sure," Kim said.

"See, I cover Kim," Ron continued.

Kim had to hand it to Ron—he didn't give up.

"I'm backup," Ron went on explaining.

"Excuse me, Don," the king said kindly, "but I really need to speak to Miss Possible alone." King Wallace and Kim stepped toward the palace.

"That's Ron," Ron called after them. "R-O-N. Thank you."

"Well, I'm bored," Prince Wally announced to Ron. "So I'm off to ride the royal go-kart."

Ron's eyes lit up. "Go-kart?" he cried. He

held out his hands as though he were gripping a steering wheel. "Freestyle!"

Wally stopped in mid-stride and turned around. "Oh, um. Would you like to come?" he asked unenthusiastically.

"Dude, I'm all about go-karts," Ron gushed.

Wally wrinkled his nose and sighed. "Very well," he said.

Apparently, the prince was too well bred to tell Ron to get lost.

CHAPTER 3

Dark and Stormy Knights

"So what's this all about, Your Majesty?" Kim asked as she followed King Wallace into a large room.

"I have a problem," the king confessed. "A terrible, ancient problem." He gestured to the large tapestry that hung on the wall behind him.

Kim looked carefully at the tapestry. It looked very old, and depicted an enormous, brutal-looking king on a throne, looking

down at a peasant at his feet. "Ancient?" Kim repeated.

"It all started centuries ago, with our first king," King Wallace explained. "Unfortunately, my ancestor ruled the kingdom with cruel arrogance."

Kim looked up at the tapestry, trying to imagine the scene.

"Please, Highness, my entire flock ran away . . . and I need a few days to pay me taxes," the peasant begged.

The king bit into a turkey leg. He chewed, then belched and tossed away the bone. "Cry

me a moat," the king said. *"Off to the tower with you."*

Kim could imagine the royal guards dragging the peasant away. . . .

"He was despised by his subjects," King Wallace went on.  "Particularly his own knights— the Knights of Rodeghan. They were determined to dethrone him. Secret plans were drafted . . . but they failed. The grudge was passed down from generation to generation. Even today, the descendants of the knights are still out there, still plotting to end the royal lineage."

"Well, if your royal family has been okay for all these generations, what's the problem now?" Kim asked.

King Wallace looked uncomfortable. "You

have met my son . . . 'Weak Link Wally,' as the press has so cruelly dubbed him."

"Oh . . ." Kim said, nodding, "yeah."

That explained everything.

In the go-kart garage, Wally stood by his vehicle, wearing a white racing jumpsuit.

"Can I wear these?" Ron asked, holding up an identical jumpsuit.

Wally gasped. "A commoner, wearing my racing togs?" he said.

"Eww," Ron said, wrinkling his nose. "No. Not your togs . . . just your clothes."

"I suppose I could just have them burned

later," Wally said as he pulled on his helmet.

"Yeah, baby!" Ron cried, zipping himself into the jumpsuit and yanking on a helmet. "Let's ride." He climbed into the go-kart and roared out of the garage behind the prince.

Racing through the course, Ron made a sharp turn, knocking Rufus out of the car. The little naked mole rat grabbed the spoiler and held on for dear life.

Suddenly, the road branched in two. Ron took the path on the right.

"Ta-ta, common Ron!" Wally shouted as he swerved down the path on the left.

"It's good to be royalty!" Ron cried as he put his foot down on the accelerator. "You get go-karts!"

Back in the palace, Kim and the King were still looking at the tapestry.

"I just can't believe that there are knights in this day and age," Kim said.

"Oh, they're quite modern," the king assured her. "They have a Web site."

Kim grinned. "A Web site?"

"They have embraced the twenty-first century," King Wallace said. "And they are more determined now than ever to abolish the monarchy."

"Well, no offense, Your Majesty," Kim said slowly, "but how do you know that this Web site is really run by these knights? It could be hackers playing a prank."

"No," the king said firmly. "I fear for my son."

Just then, a scream echoed through the palace.

Kim and the king raced outside. Ron's go-kart was swerving all over the course in front of the palace—as laser blasts exploded on the ground around him!

Ron turned the wheel sharply to avoid another blast. "Aggghhh!" he cried.

"Wade!" Kim called as she activated the Kimmunicator. "Come in, Wade!"

Wade appeared on the screen. He was wearing pajamas, and looked pretty grumpy. "Do you have any idea what time it is here?" Wade demanded.

"Are you picking up any aircraft in this area?" Kim asked, ignoring his question.

Wade peered at one of the many monitors around him. "Nope. My scans show nothing."

"Scan higher," Kim commanded. "There's gotta be something."

Wade tapped at his keyboard. "Hey, that's weird," he said, rubbing his chin.

Kim peered at the screen intently. "What?"

"I'm picking up a satellite in geosynchronous orbit," Wade explained.

"Government? Military?" Kim asked.

"Private," Wade said. "Some company called Rodeghan Industries."

"The Knights of Rodeghan," Kim whispered to herself. "I need the Kimmunicator to broadcast a scramble signal," she told Wade.

Ron continued weaving across the track, dodging beams as they exploded all around him. Both he and Rufus were screaming their heads off.

Kim took a running leap and managed to catch the tail of the go-kart. "Stop!" she shouted to Ron as the Kimmunicator let out a low whine—it was broadcasting the signal.

"You got it, K.P.!" Ron cried, hitting the brake.

Wade's voice crackled over the Kimmunicator. "The laser fire should stop about . . . now!"

Sure enough, the blasts stopped.

"Hey!" Ron said, smiling.

Kim heaved a sigh of relief. "You rock in stereo, Wade."

Wade yawned. "Can I go back to sleep now?" he asked.

Suddenly, Kim and Ron saw the king running toward them. "Wally? Where's my son?" he yelled.

Just then, Wally zoomed up in his go-kart. He had a cup of tea in his hand. "Teatime!" Wally chirped.

"Oh, thank heavens," the king said. "Oh. You see, Miss Possible, I have urgent need of your services. You simply must stay."

Kim shook her head. "Can't."

"But my son is not safe here!" King Wallace insisted.

"But I have to get back to school for the election," Kim explained.

"What's an election?" Wally asked as he climbed out of his go-kart.

"Something we'll lose if we don't get back on the campaign trail," Ron said.

"I've got it!" King Wallace exclaimed. "What say Wally tag along with you?"

Kim and Ron gaped at each other.

"America is so much larger than our land," the king went on. "It would be a perfect place to hide."

Kim hesitated, giving Wally a sideways glance. She didn't really want him to come back with her. Then again, if anything happened to him here, she'd feel responsible. "Well . . ." she said.

Wally clapped his hands eagerly. "Oooh! Is your crib in a 'hood?" he asked brightly. "Oh! That could be quite exhilarating!"

Kim rolled her eyes. This was going to be *some* foreign exchange.

CHAPTER 4

Prince Smarming

"Oh, Mrs. Possible!" Wally singsonged as he held up a plate heaped with delicate little cucumber sandwiches.

Kim rolled her eyes.

Kim's mom made a sour face and sing-songed back, "Yeeee-ees."

Wally was sitting next to Kim at the Possible breakfast table. He had only been there for a few hours, but he was already working every Possible nerve.

"My cucumber sandwiches must have the crusts removed before they are presented to me," Wally said, frowning at the plate. He picked up a sandwich and gave it a disapproving sniff.

Kim's mom grabbed her daughter by the elbow and dragged her into the next room. "Kim!" she cried warningly.

"Mom, I know," Kim said sympathetically. "But Wally won't be here long. Just till he's out of danger."

"Oh, Mrs. Possible!" Wally cooed again.

Shooting a final glare at her daughter, Kim's mom trudged off to tend to the prince.

* * *

Later that morning, Kim sighed as she walked toward Middleton High. It was bad enough that the school's billboard read PICK BRICK in huge letters (and "Paid for by Bonnie Rockwaller" in smaller ones), but now Kim was going to have to spend her day showing around Wally, the Royal Pain.

"Please," Wally begged. "I beseech you, let me wear my own garments, not these, ew, commoner rags!" Wally was dressed in cargo pants and a T-shirt that Ron had lent him.

"You're keeping a low profile, remember?" Kim said.

Just then, two girls walked past them.

"There he is!" one of the girls

shouted. "Prince Wally!" she cooed, waving.

Just then, Kim caught sight of the mob in front of the school. There were students, teachers, a news van, and a reporter . . . all waiting for Prince Wally.

"Excuse me," Ron said, elbowing his way through the crowd. "Pardon me. Pardon me." Ron reached the center of the crowd and held up his hands. "Everyone, please listen up. The press conference will begin shortly."

Kim yanked Ron to the side. "Press

conference?" she whispered fiercely. "What part of 'low profile' don't you understand?"

"Kim," Ron said patiently, "your campaign needs a boost."

"Are you going to go on again about how popular Brick is?" Kim demanded.

Ron gave her a knowing grin. "Oh, sure, he's popular. But he doesn't have a prince about to endorse him . . . on TV," he said.

The crowd let out a cheer. Kim turned and saw that Wally was already talking to the reporter.

"It's not every day the sleepy little town of

Middleton plays host to royalty," the reporter said into the camera. "Prince Wally was kind enough to grant us an interview." She faced Wally. "Your Highness, we were told you wanted to endorse someone for the school's upcoming election." The reporter held out the microphone.

Wally blinked. "Hmm?" he asked blankly. "Oh, yes, yes," he said, pointing toward Kim. "That one over there, Kim something or other. A bit high-strung to ever be a world-class leader, but, um . . . hmm, but perfectly adequate for public high school."

Kim gritted her teeth. Some endorsement, she thought sarcastically.

The reporter laughed. "Perhaps you think

you'd make a better class president?" she asked the prince.

"Well, naturally," Wally said. "I have been groomed for greatness."

The reporter smiled and asked, "Are you saying you would be a better class president than Kim Possible?"

"No, no, no, no, I'm not saying that," Wally said quickly.

Kim heaved a sigh of relief.

Wally grinned. "Because it goes without saying."

The reporter and the crowd laughed.

Kim clenched her fists. She wanted to send Wally right back home—Express Mail.

"Hmm . . ." Wally said, stroking his chin. "Perhaps I shall toss my crown into the ring, after all."

The crowd murmured with excitement as the reporter rushed over to Kim. "Kim Possible, you're running against royalty. How does it feel?" she asked.

Kim grabbed the microphone from the reporter. "I relish the competition!" she growled. "After all, that's what democracy is all about. Earning the right to lead."

"Unless, of course, one has the birthright to lead," Wally countered.

"There you have it, folks," the reporter said into the camera. "Middleton High is in for a battle royal. Who will win: the prince or the pauper?"

* * *

"Pauper?" Kim screeched as she stared at the television later that night.

"I believe she was referring to you," Wally said from his place on the couch next to her. He was lounging in a bathrobe embroidered with the crown logo. The whole family—

plus Ron—had gathered to watch Kim and Wally on the TV news.

Wally stretched and stood up. "Well, I shall consider my campaign strategy while lounging in the bath. Um . . . excuse me," he said, eyeing the group on the couch. "Who plans to draw it this evening?"

Kim's family stared angrily at the prince.

"Perhaps *you*, Mrs. Possible?" Wally suggested. "You haven't been pulling your weight around here of late."

Kim's mom looked like she was about to lose it. "Arggh!"

"Wally, I think we need to have a little talk about how we do things in the land of the free," Kim's dad said.

"Blah, blah, blah," Wally said as he thrust a bottle of bubble bath into Mr. Possible's hand. "Talk is cheap." He held up three fingers. "Three drops. Not two. Not four. And then sprinkle this lavender," he added, handing his host another bottle. "Mmm. You are a good man, and true."

Kim's dad growled in response, but he could see there was no point in arguing with Wally. He trudged off to draw the bath.

"I suppose I'll need some posters and buttons and such," Wally said, thinking about his campaign. He turned to Kim. "You'll get on that, of course."

"Uh, no," Kim snapped. "You shouldn't

even be running at all. You weren't even nominated."

Wally gasped. "Oh, I see. You feel threatened. I will gladly withdraw, if that's what you want," he said.

Ron leaped from the couch, his eyes wide. "But that's not what the people want!" he pleaded.

Kim lifted her eyebrows. "Those same two guys in the caf?"

"Yes," Ron said, nodding. "And Brick is yesterday's news."

Kim brightened. Well, that was good to hear, at least. "Really?" she asked.

"Totally," Ron chirped. "It's Wally all the way. I've got it all planned out. But we have to get started immediately, because the Possible campaign is way ahead of us."

Kim stared at Ron. Is he serious? she

thought. "The 'Possible Campaign'?" Kim repeated. "You're my campaign manager."

Ron winced. "Yeah, about that," he said. "It's like a conflict of interest." Ron put his arm on Wally's shoulder. "Good luck, Kim." Ron and Wally strode out of the room.

"I'll just run my own campaign!" Kim shouted after them, furious. "With less golfing!"

Then the Kimmunicator let out its familiar chirp. "Hey, Wade," Kim said as she looked at the screen. "What's the sitch?"

"I checked out Rodeghan's Web site," Wade said.

"And?"

"I found something," Wade said, sounding confused. "But I can't figure out what it means: 'The tapestry holds the truth.'"

Kim thought for a moment. "Hmm." Then she snapped her fingers. "There was a tapestry in the palace," she said.

She needed to call King Wallace—right away.

CHAPTER 5

Big Ears, Small Brain

Kim stood in the middle of a large, state-of-the-art laboratory, wearing goggles and a white lab coat. The tapestry was hanging on the wall. King Wallace's voice sounded over the Kimmunicator.

"I assure you, Miss Possible," the king said, "my best people have examined the tapestry. They found nothing."

"Can't hurt to double-check," Kim said quickly. "Thanks for shipping it over so fast.

I'll I.M. you if I find anything. Bye." She put down the Kimmunicator and turned to face her dad, who was standing behind a glass barrier, also in a white lab coat.

"All right, Kimmie," her father said cheerfully, "we're ready to run the sequence."

"Great!" Kim grinned. "Thanks for letting me use your lab, Dad."

Kim's father punched a few buttons. "Hey, what's federal funding for?" he said.

A mechanical arm dropped from the ceiling. A beam of light shot from it and projected onto the tapestry.

"See anything?" Dr. Possible asked.

Awaiting the light of a full harvest moon, Rodeghan's foe will soon face his DOOM...

Kim peered at the tapestry. "Hmm. Nothing yet," she said. She leaned in closer. "Hold up. There's something there. Can you widen the beam?"

"Sure thing," Dr. Possible said as he hit some more buttons and the beam widened across the entire face of the tapestry.

Suddenly, the beam of light caught something—silvery, ancient-looking writing.

"'Awaiting the light of a full harvest moon, Rodeghan's foe will soon face his doom,'" Kim read. The words sent a shiver down her spine. "'In the shadow of the palace we will not be deterred. . . .'"

* * *

"'The monarchy ends with Wallace the Third,'" Kim finished. It was the next day, and she was sitting in the cafeteria across from Wally and Ron.

Wally gave Kim a dubious look. "So, for my own good, I should keep a 'low profile'?" he asked, his voice dripping with sarcasm.

"Guys, this is serious," Kim replied, her eyes flashing dangerously. "Wally, you are definitely the target. And next week's a full moon."

Wally didn't look impressed. "Hmm," he

49

 said. "Next week also happens to be the election which you would like very much to win." His eyes narrowed. "Wouldn't you?"

How can a prince with such big ears be so bad at listening? Kim thought.

Ron leaned toward Wally. "She's trying to get you to stop campaigning," he said.

Kim sighed heavily. "Will you forget about the election?"

"Oh, you'd like that, wouldn't you?" Ron asked, gesturing toward Kim with his sandwich.

"I would like to save him from the Knights of Rodeghan!" Kim cried.

"Miss Possible," Wally said in a bored voice, "this 'prophecy' clearly states that I must be in the shadow of the palace. Now, do you see the palace? I don't."

Kim pressed her lips together. "That's true, I guess," she admitted.

Wally stood up and turned to face the rest of the cafeteria. "Farewell, all!" he called, giving the crowd a princely wave. "I'm off to biology class."

"Bye!" the students chorused. "Ta-ta!"

Kim watched him go. She buried her head in her arms. *I can't believe I'm losing to this guy,* she thought. *I've got to do something—and fast!*

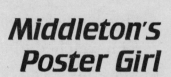

CHAPTER 6

Middleton's Poster Girl

"Uote for me, Kim P.!" Kim said as she handed a button, with a picture of herself on it, to a guy from her math class.

The guy winced and held out a crown-shaped button bearing Wally's image. "Sorry, I'm already voting for Prince Wally," he said.

Kim dropped her button back in the basket. Geez, she thought, it looks like the Possible campaign has really fallen behind.

* * *

That afternoon, Kim dashed into the gym in her cheerleading uniform. She was late because she had been busy designing a cool new campaign poster. "Hey, guys!" Kim called as she hurried to join the rest of the squad.

But the cheer squad wasn't paying attention. In fact, they weren't even looking in her direction. Instead, they were all staring at a giant mural that covered the entire gym wall. Prince Wally's larger-than-life picture grinned down at them.

"Wally . . ." one of the cheerleaders said, and the rest sighed dreamily.

Kim stared at the mural. I think I'm going to need a new poster, she thought.

* * *

But it wasn't just the Middleton High School election that was heating up. Two mysterious men in sleek black suits and dark sunglasses stepped off a plane and into the Middleton

Customs office. Each of the men carried a steel suitcase. They both slapped their passports down in front of the Customs official.

The Customs official frowned. "Is this a country?" he asked, staring at the passports. "I've never heard of it." Nonetheless, the Customs official stamped both passports and handed them back.

"You will," one of them snarled.

Then he and the other man stalked off.

"Welcome to Middleton!" the Customs official called after them, waving.

Ron and Wally stood on the fourth hole at the Middleton Mini-Golf course—the site of the famous Old Faithful obstacle. Every few minutes, the geyser in the middle of the hole exploded into a huge fountain of hot water. Basically, you wanted to get your ball in the hole before the scalding water went off, totally drenching you.

"Your Highness," Ron said, "maybe we've pushed the 'royal' angle too much."

Wally gasped. "Bite your tongue!" he cried.

"Okay, sure," Ron said with a shrug. "Being a prince is how you got the voters' attention. But now they seem to actually like you."

Wally lifted his eyebrows. "As a person?"

The prince and the campaign manager stared at each other for a moment. Then they cracked up.

After all, who could possibly like Wally as a person?

Just then, the ground began to shake. Red mercury in the huge thermometer planted next to the geyser began to rise. Bells clanged, and suddenly, a tower of boiling hot water spewed up out of the ground.

Wally jumped into Ron's arms.

At the same time, Kim tiptoed down the dark

hallway of Middleton High School. She was wearing an all-black outfit, and her hair was tied back in a ponytail. Kim hurried over to the bulletin board. This mission required speed and stealth. After all, she didn't want to get caught slapping her campaign posters over Wally's.

Kim pasted up her poster and moved onto the next.

Then her Kimmunicator went off.

"Hey, Wade," Kim said.

"How's it going?" Wade asked.

"I'm all over it," Kim said, narrowing her

eyes intensely. "I'm putting up oomphier posters and I've been focus-testing my new hair." Kim ran her hand over her ponytail. "Voters wanted it pulled back. What do you think?"

"I mean since the prince was on TV," Wade clarified, frowning. "Do you think the Knights of Rodeghan know he's in Middleton?"

A strand of hair popped out of the front of Kim's ponytail, and she smoothed it back into place. "Dunno," she said absently. The strand refused to settle back down.

"The prophecy mentioned a full moon," Wade said impatiently.

Kim rummaged around in her bag and pulled out a small bottle of hair spray. She spritzed her hair back into place and smoothed it down. "Sure did," she said.

"Tonight's a full moon," Wade pointed out.

The hair popped out of place again, and Kim sighed. "Yeah," she said, pulling the elastic from her hair and shaking it out, "but it's like Wally said, he's nowhere near the palace. No palace, no prophecy."

Wade looked intently at Kim. "Where is he now?" he asked.

Kim shrugged as she fiddled with her hair. Why is Wade so bent out of shape about this? she wondered. Doesn't he see that I've got important campaign matters to worry about? "I'm guessing miniature golfing with his campaign manager . . ." Kim said, then stopped. "At Middleton Mini-Golf . . ." she continued slowly. Suddenly, an image of the golf course flashed in her mind. "The sixth hole—it's a palace!"

CHAPTER 7

Mini-Golf Is
a Total Blast

"**W**here's that caddy?" Wally demanded.

Wally and Ron turned and saw Rufus struggling toward them. He was lugging their putters behind him, muttering all the way.

Wally picked up his putter and took aim at the fifth-hole obstacle—the Head of the Sphinx. He gave the ball a firm whack, hitting it directly into the hole below the Sphinx's head.

"Yes!" Wally cried as the Sphinx lit up.

61

But, suddenly, the Sphinx spit out the ball, which came rolling back down the putting green. "Hey!" Wally cried. He strode over to the Sphinx and pointed at it dramatically. "By royal decree, I demand a do-over!"

At that moment, the Sphinx head exploded, splintering into a million pieces. An enormous figure dressed in armor, holding a staff, rose out of the smoke and dust.

Wally, Ron, and Rufus screamed as a Knight of Rodeghan came near.

Just then, Kim Possible landed lightly between the knight and her friends. "I can't allow you to smash my presidential opponent!" she cried. Kim didn't waste any time.

She kicked the knight, knocking him down.

"Oh, thank goodness you've arrived!" Wally cried. "Does this mean I can leave?"

Kim pointed behind Wally, where another knight, holding an ancient-looking barbed mace, was charging at them.

"Aaahh!" Ron yelled. "A pointy-ball stick!"

The mace glowed purple, and an instant later, a laser blast erupted from one of the barbs, exploding over the friends' heads.

"Laser pointy-ball stick!" Ron shouted as he, Kim, and Wally started to run. Lasers blasted the ground near their feet.

The Knights of Rodeghan began to advance. "Awaiting the light of a full harvest moon, Rodeghan's foe will soon face his doom," they chanted.

Wally and Ron were shaking with fear beside Kim. Suddenly, Kim glanced up and saw the full moon. And it was harvest time, too. She had to break the prophecy!

"In the shadow of the palace, it will not be deterred," the knights went on. "The monarchy ends with Wallace the Third."

"Well . . ." Wally said, trying to crawl away, "as you know, I am known far and wide as Wally, so surely—"

The first knight slammed his staff down in front of Wally, blocking his path. The knight reached down to grab the prince, who whimpered in terror. Suddenly, a cable shot out, coiling around the knight's hand. The cable jerked the knight's hand back with a vicious yank. Surprised, the knight turned to see Kim at the other end of the cable.

"Leave him alone," Kim commanded.

The knight sneered at Kim. "This is none of your concern, little girl," he said as he gave the cable a yank, jerking Kim onto the ground.

Ron watched the scene, wide-eyed. "The voters will not like this," he said.

Rufus handed Ron a putter, and Ron threw it toward Kim, shouting, "Kim, catch!"

Kim leaped to her feet and snatched the club. She held it in the air as she faced the knight who stood over Wally.

Suddenly, Kim felt a tap on her shoulder. When she turned, she saw the second knight. He was holding up his laser-mace, grinning evilly.

Quick as lightning, Kim shot a grappling hook overhead, hooking it onto a large tree. Kim soared into the sky on the cable as the knight blasted away with his mace.

"Be careful with that thing!" the first knight shouted. He'd been lightly toasted with a stray laser.

"Oops," said the second knight.

The first knight looked down and hauled Wally to his feet. "Now about you," he said.

"Please!" Wally begged. "My father will give you anything! Whatever you want!" Wally's nose began to run as he burst into sobs.

Meanwhile, Ron and Rufus had sneaked over to the eighth hole, which sat at the top of a nearby hill. Hole eight featured the *Titanic*. Or, rather, half of the *Titanic*—it was made to look as if the other half was sunken into the

ground. Ron picked up a putter, and with some help from Rufus, started digging up the ship. It soon began to come loose. "The *Titanic*'s going down . . . again!" Ron cried as he and Rufus pushed the half-ship down the hill toward the knights.

"Gold!" Wally said to the knight. "Jewels! Just speak the word, and I will grant you—"

Just then, the *Titanic* swept past, taking the knight with it. Wally stood blinking at the empty space where the knight had stood only moments before. "—nothing," he finished. "On second thought, I will grant you nothing."

The *Titanic* came to a stop. Then it seemed to rise out of the earth. With a desperate heave, the knight lifted the ship over his head and tossed it away.

Wally fell to his knees and started blubbering again. "Please, I'll give you anything—yah!"

Just then, from out of nowhere, a cable shot out and coiled around the prince's waist. It pulled him into a tree, where he disappeared among the leaves.

"Shh!" Kim said to Wally as she removed the cable from his belt and attached it to her own. She'd be needing that grappling hook again. "Stay here," she said. "And be quiet."

Kim dove from the branch and did a triple-flip to land lightly on a fiberglass windmill. The knights gaped at her.

"The prophecy never mentioned her," the first knight said uncertainly.

Kim folded her arms across her chest and frowned grimly. "Prophecy schmophecy."

Running forward, the knight used his staff to catapult himself onto the windmill. But Kim was too fast. She dropped from the side of the structure and grabbed onto one of the turning blades. As the blade rose, she landed a heavy kick to the knight's stomach.

"Aggh!" the knight cried as he flew from the top of the windmill and dropped to the ground with a brutal thud.

"Maybe you should rethink this whole career choice," said Kim.

"That's it," the other knight said, taking aim at the windmill with his laser-mace. "No more Mr. Nice Knight!"

A laser ripped from the mace in a brilliant burst of light. The windmill exploded, leaving only a smoking, charred mess. "All too easy," the knight said, grinning.

A groan sounded behind him.

The knight turned and saw Kim clinging onto the Leaning Tower of Pisa—the featured attraction of hole thirteen. Kim had taken a flying leap just as the blast hit the windmill, and the force had blown her clear across the course. She clutched at the tower desperately. She was about to fall!

CHAPTER 8

Faithful Old Faithful

"Give it up, girl," the knight growled at Kim.

At that moment, the ground began to rumble. Kim took a diving leap from the tower and landed on the green behind Old Faithful.

Just a little closer, Kim thought as the knight headed her way.

The knight ignored the obstacle as Old Faithful's bell began to clang and the mercury began to rise. "We don't want you, we only want the prince," the knight said.

At that moment, the geyser exploded with a staggering force, erupting directly under the knight. It thrust him into the air, sending him sailing across the sky.

"Yaaahhh!" the knight cried as he landed hard on the plastic turf.

Quickly, Ron ripped up a piece of turf and folded it over the knight, then gave the knight a shove with his foot. The knight spun downhill, wrapped snugly in the turf.

"Boo-yah!" Ron shouted.

It only took twenty minutes for the Middleton police to arrive, and when they did, they didn't believe Kim's story.

"So, you expect me to believe that these 'knights' came to Middleton Mini-Golf to carry out some kind of ancient-prophecy-type deal?" Officer Hobble asked, looking skeptical.

Kim peered over to where another police-man was leading the knights toward the squad car.

"Officer, I can't make this stuff up," Kim said.

Ron sneaked behind the officer and peered over his shoulder to see what he was writing. "Did you get the part about me in there?" he asked, tapping on the officer's notepad.

The officer looked disapprovingly at Ron. "Vandalism to the mini *Titanic*?" he asked.

Ron grinned. "And my name again is Barkin," he said, naming the teacher from Middleton High School. "That's B-A-R . . ."

Kim looked over to where Wally was still

perched up in his tree. He finally hopped down, and Kim walked over to join him.

"Kim Possible," Wally said, taking her hand. "You saved my life." Kim thought it was the first time that his voice actually didn't sound snooty.

"No big," Kim said with a shrug. "Just doing the teen hero thing."

"No," Wally said, shaking his head. "You are a true leader. You have my vote."

Kim's face brightened. "Well," she said with a smile, "that's at least *two* votes."

CHAPTER 9

The Student Formerly Known as Prince

"All right," Mr. Barkin said as he stood at the podium in front of the school.

Kim shifted in her seat. They were about to hear the election results, and according to Ron's exit polls, it was Wally all the way.

"That's two votes for Kim Possible," Mr. Barkin announced.

Kim blinked. Two? How embarrassing. She hunched lower in her seat.

"Zero votes for Brick Flagg," Mr. Barkin went on.

Kim sat up a little straighter. Okay, so the most popular jock in school got zero votes—she suddenly didn't feel as bad.

"Nine hundred and ninety-eight for Prince Wally," Mr. Barkin finished.

The crowd erupted into cheers as Brick pounded Wally on the back. "You had my vote, dude!" Brick shouted. "Way to go!"

Kim glared at Ron. This was all his fault. If he hadn't tried to get the prince to endorse her in the election, she'd be giving her "My Fellow Middletonians" speech right now.

Ron shrugged and gave Kim a sheepish smile. "The guy has leadership experience. He's very good at giving orders," he said.

Wally stepped over to Kim. "Well, this was quite an invigorating race," he said.

Kim folded her arms across her chest. "It sure was."

Suddenly, King Wallace bounded onstage and wrapped Wally in a tight hug. "Congratulations, son," he said.

"Daddy!" Wally squealed. "You made it!"

"I wouldn't miss it for the world!" King Wallace said warmly. "Now we must go home so that you may continue to prepare to take over the crown."

Wally bit his lip. "Yes, actually, Daddy," he said seriously, "there's something I've been meaning to speak to you about. I've decided that, after you retire, I'd like to run for president of our land."

King Wallace frowned. "Presidents don't get to wear the day coat with the ermine trim," he reminded his son.

Wally gasped. "Hadn't thought of that." He glanced at Kim and said, "Oh, well. Sacrifices must be made. This contest has shown me that democracy is, as my Middleton peeps would say, 'bon diggity.'"

"Democracy?" King Wallace repeated. "But that means no more kings."

"The prophecy!" Ron cried, his eyes wide. "'The monarchy ends with Wallace the Third.' It came true!"

King Wallace rubbed his chin. "So it has."

"Cool," Kim said, patting Wally on the

back. "Now you can go home and show the democracy thing." And I can be class president, she thought, since I came in second!

"No, Kim," Wally said, shaking his head seriously. "I've decided to stay in Middleton and finish my term as class president." He clenched his fists in excitement.

"That's great," Kim said through gritted teeth. "Just. Great." Oh well, she told herself, look on the bright side—at least Ron will have someone to go mini-golfing with!